WISE OWL TALES · STORIES OF A SHARED PLANET

To Brooklyn,
Happy Reading!
Dr Buer

Wise Owl Tales are written in rhyme,
Of animal friends who need our time.

Realistic fiction, stories told,
In nature's settings, tales unfold.

For thoughtful people who understand,
To help the animals, we need a plan.

Books for readers, young to old,
The future of the world we hold.

Our planet Earth is what we share,
Wise Owl Tales, for those who care.

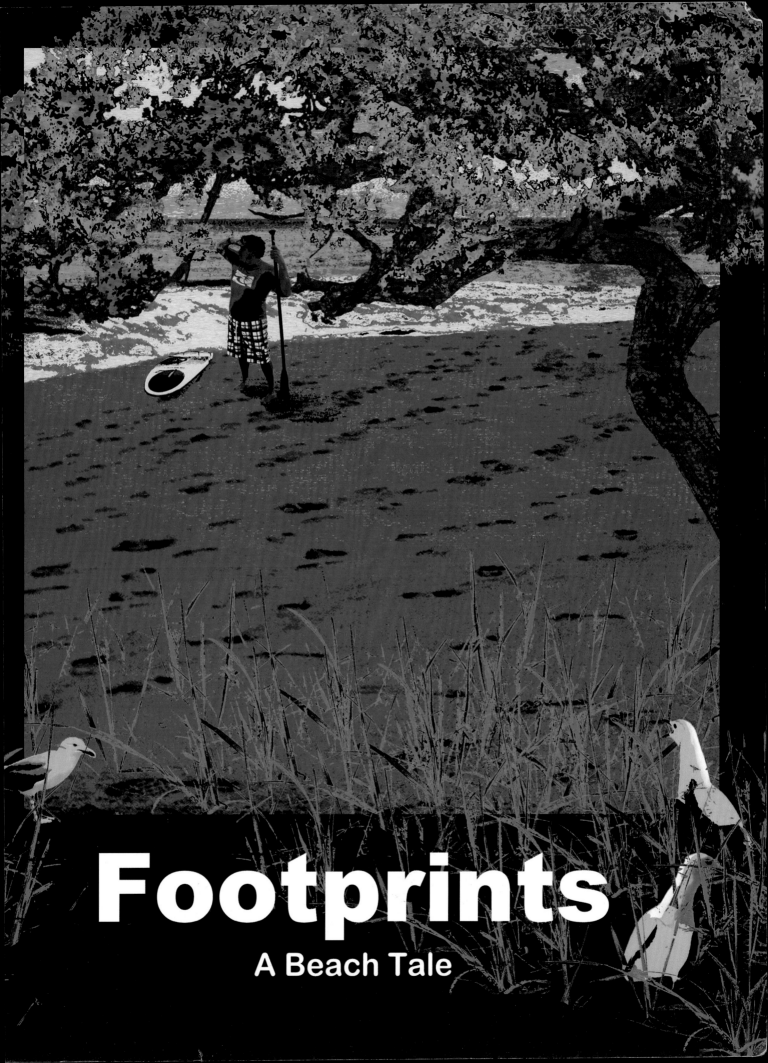

Footprints

A Beach Tale

Whose footprints in the sand are these,
Between the surf and ocean breeze?

Down on the beach, horizon grand,
That magic place where sea meets land.

Who left these tracks just where they please,
To whom do we belong, they tease?

Whose footprints in the sand are these,
Between the surf and ocean breeze?

Who left these tracks just where they please,
To whom do we belong, they tease?

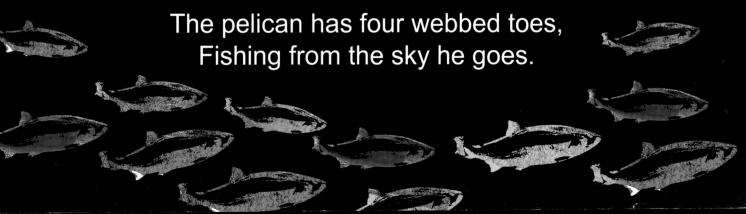

The pelican has four webbed toes,
Fishing from the sky he goes.

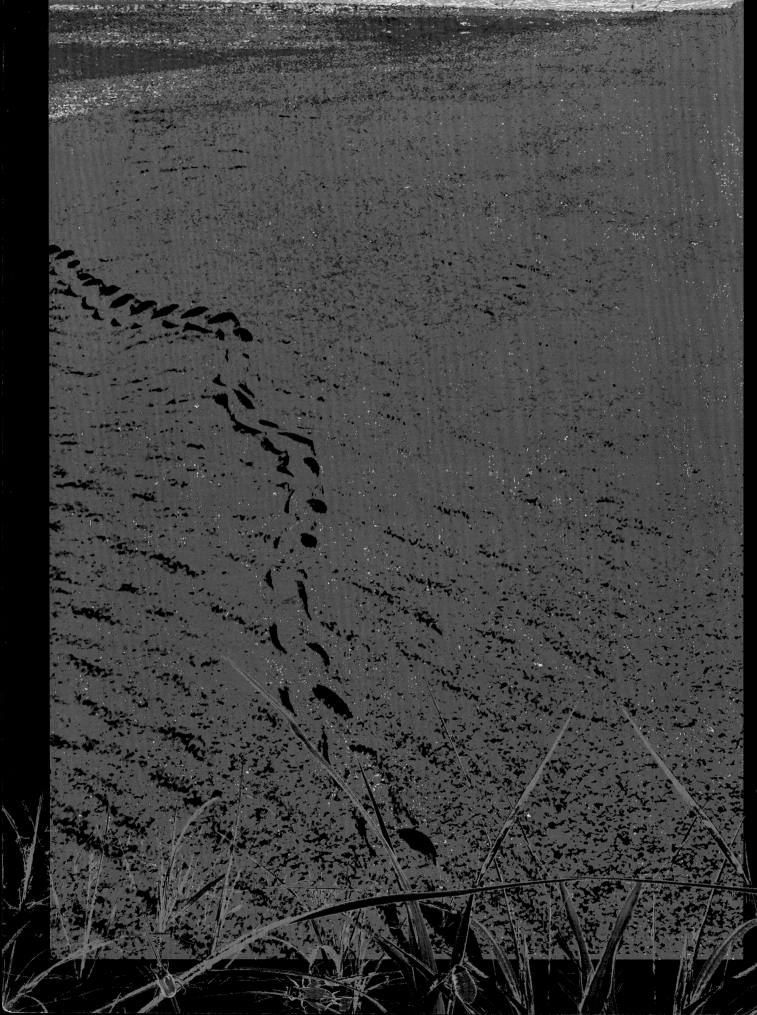

Whose footprints in the sand are these,
Between the surf and ocean breeze?

A curving line without a break,
A trail is left behind the snake.

Who left these tracks just where they please,
To whom do we belong, they tease?

Back and forth sandpipers run,
Their search for food is never done.

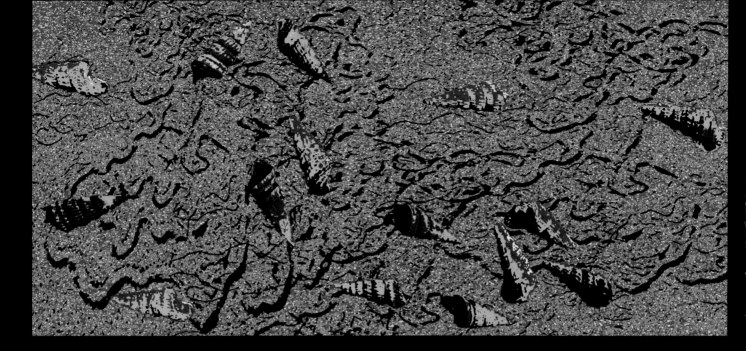

Whose footprints in the sand are these,
Between the surf and ocean breeze?

A spiral home has the snail,
He leaves behind a slimy trail.

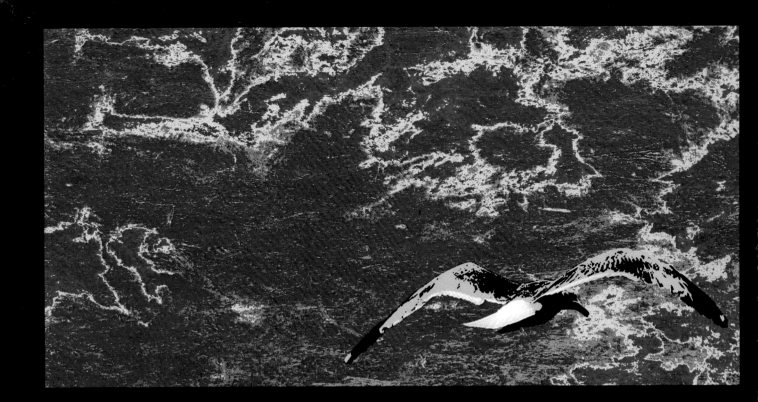

Who left these tracks just where they please,
To whom do we belong, they tease?

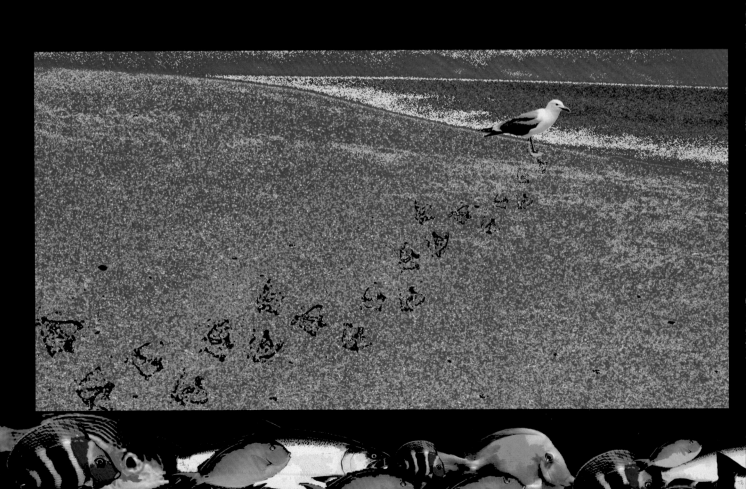

The seagulls call with a loud squawk,
To nests along the beach they flock.

Whose footprints in the sand are these,
Between the surf and ocean breeze?

Some are so small they're hard to see,
Close to the waves, the tiny flea.

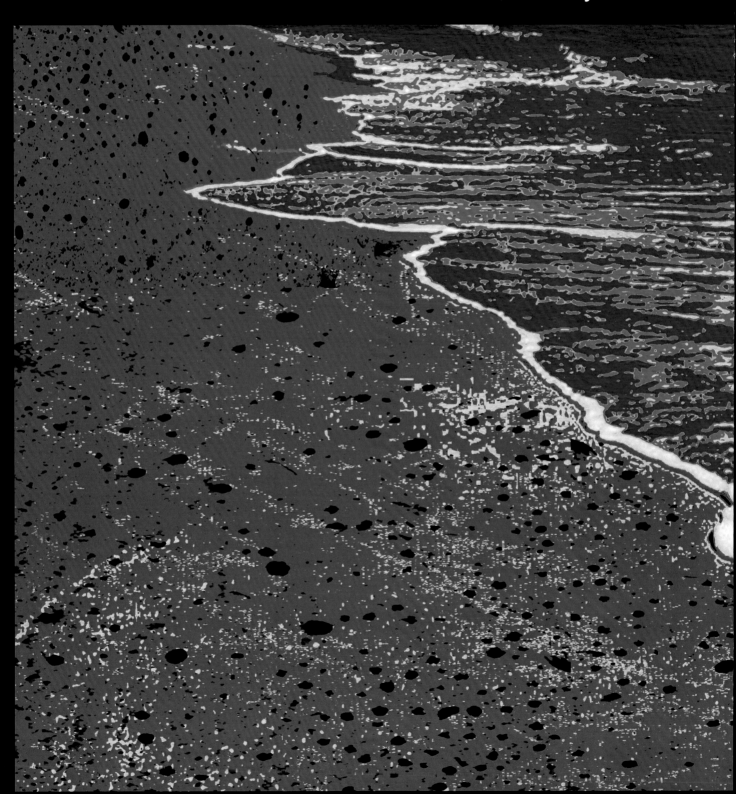

Who left these tracks just where they please,
To whom do we belong, they tease?

The vulture keeps the beaches clean,
A scavenger, his eyes are keen.

Whose footprints in the sand are these,
Between the surf and ocean breeze?

Loud and gruff, sea lions bark,
Basking in the sun till dark.

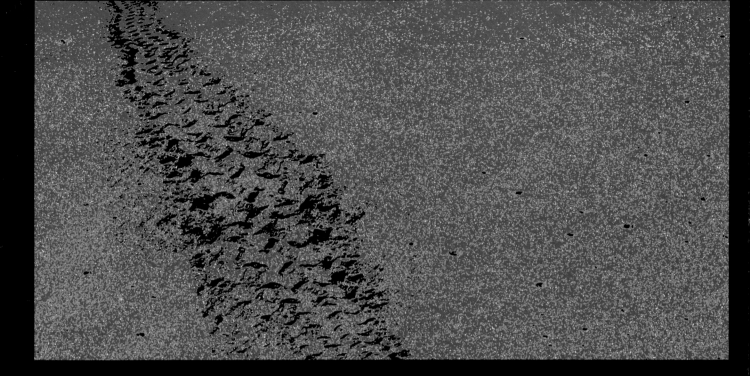

Who left these tracks just where they please,
To whom do we belong, they tease?

Returning to the beach at night,
The turtle hides her eggs from sight.

Whose footprints in the sand are these,
Between the surf and ocean breeze?

Catching frisbees in the air,
Dogs on the beach without a care!

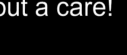

Splashing, playing with a friend,
A day together we will spend.

Footprints belong to people, too,
Barefoot, sandal, running shoe.

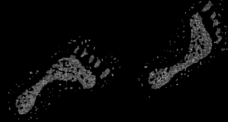

Some are in groups, some are alone,
But each one is its very own.

The tide rolls in along the shore,
Erasing tracks forever more.

The beach awaits as waves cascade,
For more footprints to be made.

Down on the beach, horizon grand,
Leave only footprints in the sand.

North America

Equator

South America

Antarctica

Dedicated to the
Beach Lovers of the World

Beach Locations and Description

Beaches are found all over the world where land meets the water of an ocean or lake creating a shoreline. They are made of sand, stones, gravel or rocks that have been deposited by the tide or waves.

Beaches can be many colors, ranging from white to black with a variety of shades in between. Over millions of years the action of the waves wears down rocks on land and the ocean floor, resulting in sand particles of varying sizes. The color of the sand is a reflection of the rocks surrounding the shoreline.

Glossary
and
Beach Facts

beach - a stretch of shoreline where land meets an ocean or lake; beaches are a diverse habitat and can be impacted by both natural and man-made events

crab - sand crabs, also called ghost crabs because of their pale coloring, dig burrows in the sand and eat small clams and debris; they have four pairs of walking legs and a pair of claws with one being larger than the other

dog - a four-legged, furry animal that barks and is usually kept as a pet; there are many different kinds, colors and sizes of dogs

flea - sand fleas, also called sand hoppers, are crustaceans that live in damp sand near water and jump from place to place; they are very small, usually less than one inch long; they stay buried in the sand during the day and come out at night to eat organic debris

footprint / track - a mark made by the foot or body of an animal in the sand; tracks can also be made by machines and vehicles

horizon - the appearance of a line or place in the distance where the earth and sky meet

pelican - a large bird that lives near the water; it spots fish from the air, dives into the water, scoops up the fish in his pouched bill and then eats the fish; the pelican is a strong swimmer with short legs and four webbed toes; pelicans have been around for millions of years

sandpiper - a small shore bird; it has a long, straight bill used for picking up insects and small crabs or fleas in the sand; it is very agile on the ground and runs back and forth between waves looking for food

scavenger - an animal that eats decaying matter or trash

seagull - a shore bird found in most parts of the world; it has large wings, webbed feet, a hooked bill and white or gray feathers; seagulls nest on the ground and will eat just about anything including insects, fish, seeds, plants and even trash

sea lion - related to seals but with larger ears and flippers; they can walk on all fours and live in colonies along the coastline where they eat fish, squid and clams; sea lions are very vocal and make dog-like barks

snail - a slow-moving mollusk that lives on land or in the water with a hard, spiral shell that protects its body; snails eat mostly plants or algae and leave a trail of slime behind; the slime acts as a suction and holds them, even upside down, to plants or other surfaces

snake - covered in dry, smooth scales, they shed their skin several times a year; carnivorous (meat eater) with flexible jaws that allow them to eat prey larger than their head because they swallow food whole; snakes live on every continent except Antarctica

surf - waves breaking on the shore

tide - the change in water level of the ocean caused by the gravitational pull of the moon and sun

turtle - sea turtles have powerful jaws for crushing and eating crabs and other animals with hard shells, they also eat jellyfish, seaweed and fish; they live in warm waters around the world and migrate thousands of miles to nest on the same beach where they were born; females dig a hole with their flippers, lay their eggs inside, then cover with sand; the eggs hatch after about 60 days and the baby turtles make their way to the sea

vulture - a large scavenger bird of prey with very good eyesight, strong legs, sharp beak and bald head; vultures eat remains of dead animals at any stage of decay; vulture stomach acid is so strong it kills any bacteria that might be in its food

Why do you think the place "where sea meets land" is described as magical?

The book describes footprints left behind on the sand; can you think of any other places footprints can be left behind?

Have you ever seen any animal tracks described in this story? If so, which ones and where did you see them?

Which footprint or track do you think is the easiest to identify and why?

What is the main idea of the story?

What are some other animals that might leave footprints or tracks on the beach?

What are possible positive or negative effects of both people and animals sharing the beach?

What do all of the animals in the story have in common?

Based on the facts in the story and glossary, how are some of these animals dependent on each other?

Do you think any of the animals mentioned in the story are able to live anywhere else other than near a beach?

What can people do to make the beach a better place for all animals to live?

What impact do oceans have on beaches?

What information does a footprint or track tell you about the individual animal or person who left it?

What is your favorite illustration or verse in the story and why?

Can you think of any tracks on a beach made by something that could be hazardous to animals or nature?

Compare and contrast the illustrations of the first and last pages of the story.

What does the last verse in the story, "leave only footprints in the sand" mean to you?

WISE OWL TALES STORIES OF A SHARED PLANET

Add to your Wise Owl Tale collection, here are more for your selection.
Visit us at www.wiseowltales.com for books and activities

A story of travel from here to there,
A young armadillo who goes everywhere.
Armando - an Adventurous Nine-Banded Armadillo Tale

A story of hunger and lost habitat,
A mother who hunts but avoids combat.
Chitraka - a Challenged Cheetah Tale

A story of rescue, where kids save the day,
Working together, they don't back away.
Daphina - a Freed Bottlenose Dolphin Tale

A story of creatures walking the shore,
Of tracks left behind, so fun to explore!
Footprints - a Beach Tale

A story of love and gratitude,
An adopted mutt with attitude!
Frank the Tank - an Adopted Dog Tale

A story of hope after despair,
An orphaned gorilla receives loving care.
Gamba - an Optimistic Mountain Gorilla Tale

A story of capture and desolation,
Of rescue, shelter and preservation.
Mali - a Rescued Asian Elephant Tale

A story of change and loss of home,
A hungry family on the roam.
Nanuk - a Hopeful Polar Bear Tale

Pictures and words by Lopez and Burk,
Inspired by nature, love their work.
Learners, teachers and travelers, who
Look at life from the animals' view.